Little Toad to the Rescue

Written and Illustrated by Leonard Shortall

gb Golden Press • New York

Western Publishing Company, Inc.
Racine, Wisconsin

"My boy, we'll have to face it—our little world is drying up," Old Toad told Little Toad.

They sat in the dusty vegetable garden watching the cabbage leaves curl. It really was a very serious situation, for toads cannot live unless their skin is moist.

Little Toad could feel himself beginning to dry out. He went to the shower and pulled the string. No water! It hadn't rained since the Tuesday before last, and the barrel was empty. Little Toad hurried back to Old Toad.

Old Toad looked hot and unhappy. He croaked, "Emergency measures are called for! Today my knee pains me so much I can't travel, but you, Little Toad, must go to Green Pond for water!"

Little Toad was excited. He had never been to Green Pond, which was far, far away. Grandfather showed him on the map the best way to go—all the way through the garden, in past the pine trees, across the wide road, over the long grassy field, and at last down the steep hill to the pond.

"It's a long trip, my boy, but I know you can do it," said Old Toad urgently. "Just keep away from the wicked crow, who has an appetite for toads. If you see him, run for cover as fast as you can. Now, off with you—hop to it!"

Little Toad felt very important. Grabbing the emergency buckets, he left at once.

As Little Toad went past the tomato plants, he looked up and saw fat Tomato Worm eating fresh green tomatoes.

"Hello, Tomato Worm! I'm going to get some water at Green Pond," he called.

"Herro, Ritto Toad!" Tomato Worm answered. He talked with his mouth full, spraying out chunks with every word.

Little Toad wiped pieces of tomato out of his eye. "I see you're eating. Don't let me disturb you. I'm in a hurry anyway," he said, heading toward the string bean patch.

Garden Spider was spinning a new web between two bean poles.

"Hello, Ms. Spider," called Little Toad. "I see you've moved."

"Oh, yes, just to get out of the heat," the spider answered in her soft voice. "Let me see now,—one over and one under,—then down and back again,—then all the way around," Little Toad heard her mutter to herself.

He called goodbye, but Garden Spider didn't seem to hear him. She just went on counting and spinning.

The spinach row was next, and Little Toad stopped to say hello to Stink Bug.

"It's nice of you to stop, Little Toad. I don't have too many friends," Stink Bug complained. Then he cheered up. "But, on the other hand, nobody bothers me much, especially in this hot spell."

"Yes, I see what you mean," said Little Toad politely, trying not to breathe too deeply. "Well, I must be running along, I've got an important job to do."

10

CLICK! CLICK! CLICK! Little Toad saw Click
Beetle lying on his back in the dust between the squash
plants. Each time the beetle made the clicking noise, he
snapped up into the air. Each time he snapped, he
landed on his back. CLICK! He snapped again! This
time he landed on his feet!

"Very good! A nice trick!" Little Toad exclaimed
as he rushed by.

"It's not a trick, it's the only way I can get on my
feet when I fall on my back," Click Beetle said. "And it
surprises away nosey birds," he called at Little Toad's
retreating back.

As he reached the edge of the garden, Little Toad caught sight of a big black crow in the old pine tree up ahead. His heart went BUMP! and he threw himself under a milkweed bush. He was just in time!

A wicked black shadow swept across the place where Little Toad had been standing. He could hear the great black wings flapping overhead. He tried not to listen to the crow cry, "Caw! Caw! Caw!"

Little Toad stayed very still. He didn't blink an eye.

13

When there was silence, Little Toad breathed to himself, "I'll just stay here awhile."

"Yes, do!" a sweet voice in the bush above him said. "I'm Monique, and I'll let you know when the coast is clear."

Little Toad was enchanted to see a beautiful striped caterpillar looking down at him. While he recovered from his terrible fright, he told Monique of his important mission to the pond.

"Oh, your grandfather must be most desperately dry by now. You must hurry on. I can see it's safe to go now," Monique finally assured him.

Looking carefully around, Little Toad scurried across the road.

"Hi De Ho, Toady," It was Grasshopper, who was balancing on the tip of a tall grass stem.

Little Toad had his big red bandana out and was mopping his face. "Can't stop!" he yelled. "Going to Green Pond! Water shortage!"

Grasshopper took a chew of tobacco. "Good luck," he shouted. His voice had a juicy, bubbly sound.

16

Little Toad heard a great, "YAWN. HOHUMMMMM! Pardon me!" He looked up and saw Cicada high up in the elm tree.

"I've been asleep in the ground for seventeen years, but I still can't seem to wake up!" Cicada sighed. "Perhaps what I need is a little nap."

"Don't let me keep you up. I'm just passing through," Little Toad called up into the tree, but Cicada had already begun to hum her loud buzzy hum.

"That's nice. Singing herself to sleep," Little Toad said as he continued his journey. "Well, I'll have time for sleeping when I finish my important job."

In the field ahead, Little Toad saw a fat, fuzzy, black-at-both-ends-and-orangy-brown-in-the-middle caterpillar.

"Woolly Bear! Wait for me!" Little Toad cried. "I'm going to get water for our shower at Green Pond," he said when he caught up with the caterpillar.

"Don't bother me," grumped Woolly Bear. "My orangy-brown stripe is narrow this year, so I'm getting set for a long winter." He hunched into the tall grass. "Right now it looks like rain," he called back over his shoulder.

"Well! That *is* news!" Little Toad exclaimed, looking up at the blue sky. "We surely could use it."

Little Toad passed some Painted Lady butterflies sipping from a thistle blossom in the meadow. "It looks like a shower, Ladies," he called to them.

The butterflies waved their pretty wings at Little Toad, and fluttered away across the meadow to another thistle.

"Rain is on the way, Woolly Bear said so!" Little Toad yelled, but the Painted Ladies didn't listen to him. They went on sipping nectar in the sunshine.

Little Toad told the weather news to a crowd of
Japanese beetles. Their mouths were stuffed full of
flower petals and they couldn't answer him.

"A thunderstorm is coming. Woolly Bear said so!"
he called to Bumble Bee.

"It's too hot to talk," Bumble Bee droned as he
buzzed away.

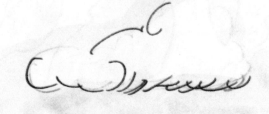

"Woolly Bear says a hurricane is almost here," Little Toad told Rhinocerous Beetle.

"Phooeey! Woolly Bear is full of hot air," the big beetle growled, shaking his black horns. He looked up at the burning sunlight, then fixed Little Toad with a stern glare.

Little Toad hurried on with his buckets.

On the hillside above Green Pond, Little Toad found Paper Wasp chewing up a willow twig to repair her nest. Wasp moved the big wad of wet willow paper to one side of her mouth, then she spoke.

"A word of warning, my young friend!" she said. "The hornets are on the warpath again. Be on the lookout for them if you are going to the pond. Heaven knows *what* their trouble is!" Little Toad watched her fly up to her nest with her mouth stuffed with paper.

"The little fellows are as mad as hornets, you might say," she called down in a muffled voice.

Close to Green Pond, Little Toad passed Cricket, who was sitting at the foot of a wild grape vine. Cricket was practicing for his nightly concert. The smell of the wild grapes and the sound of Cricket's music filled the warm air.

Little Toad's arms were growing tired from carrying the buckets, but he knew he was almost there, so he straightened his shoulders and marched along, humming Cricket's song.

He didn't see the hornets coming. But he certainly
heard them! They seemed to come from nowhere, and
in an instant they were flying around him, sounding
like a hundred buzz saws.

In four big hops Little Toad reached Green Pond.
Buckets flying, he dove into the water with a mighty
SPLASH!

Pretty soon Little Toad poked his big eyes out just above the water. He didn't see any hornets or hear any buzzing. He poked his head all the way out. The hornets had gone home.

As the waves from his splash died down, Little Toad noticed everyone heading for the end of the pond. Pushing his buckets before him, he began to swim over there. The water felt deliciously cool and wet to his parched skin.

As Little Toad reached the end of the pond, he saw
green frogs and bullfrogs and tree frogs all lined up in a
big long row. They were passing buckets of water along
the row. As they worked they chanted, "Yoho heave-
ho, yoho heave-ho," in their deep throaty voices.

Little Toad leaped out of the water and ran down the row of frogs to see what they were doing. At the end of the row he saw Ladybug and her children standing near their burning house.

"I shouldn't have left my iron on," Ladybug remarked sadly. "Pour it on the kitchen. That's right!" she directed the frogs. "Oh! What would I do without you kind neighbors?"

"I'll help, too!" cried Little Toad, and he joined the line of frogs. The kitchen was ablaze, and for a while it looked as if the fire would spread to the back porch.

But finally the fire was drenched, and Little Toad rested with the exhausted firefighters, meanwhile telling them of his important mission.

Everyone commented on how Little Toad looked like his father and grandfather, which made Little Toad puff up with pride.

Then the frogs helped Little Toad fill up his buckets with water. "We'll fill our buckets, too, and go along with you to water the garden, Little Toad!" they cried.

So each frog filled his bucket, too, and they all left for the garden.

Little Toad and the crowd of frogs made their way
up the hill from Green Pond, through the meadow, over
the road, past the pine trees, and into the vegetable
garden. As Little Toad met his bug friends, he asked
them to come to a party. Everyone said they would
come.

Everyone, that is, except Monique, whom Little Toad couldn't find. He looked all around her milkwood bush, but she wasn't there. He sat down under the bush to think. Just overhead, he saw a pale green pod dangling from the underside of a leaf. He watched it turn this way and that in the gentle wind, and then he joined the crowd again.

Old Toad was delighted to see Little Toad and all the frogs and all the buckets of water. He directed them to pour water on the plants and to fill the shower barrel.

"Little Toad," he said, "you have done a fine job!"

Little Toad felt very proud.

41

While the frogs were blowing up balloons and the other guests were hanging streamers, Little Toad wandered back to the milkweed plant with Grasshopper. All he saw was the same green pod on the leaf.

Grasshopper knew what was happening at once. "You see, Toady," he said, "Monique hasn't gone away. She's in the pod, changing from a beautiful caterpillar into a beautiful butterfly. Don't be sad, she'll be out in about a week."

"But I wanted her to come to my party," Little Toad complained.

Grasshopper understood. "Well, maybe we can break off her leaf and take her along right in the pod," he suggested. "She is asleep but at least we'll have her with us."

And that is what they did.

So they had their party, and Monique was there. Everyone had a wonderful time, except that Cicada dozed off just before the ice cream, and Click Beetle couldn't get right-side up, but he ate strawberry upside-down cake and was perfectly happy.

Finally the party was over, but Little Toad liked it so much that he said, "I know! Next week let's have a coming-out party for Monique!"

"Yes! Yes!" everyone cried, and they all went home to make their plans.

Finally Old Toad and Little Toad were alone with Monique. Old Toad was having an after-party snack.

"It's all a matter of timing, my boy," he said.

Little Toad watched as Old Toad threw a peppermint into the air.

ZAP! Old Toad's sticky tongue shot out and caught the mint on its way down. He popped it into his big mouth faster than Little Toad could say "Zip!"

"Just a simple matter of timing," Old Toad mumbled. Slowly his eyes closed. He began to snore.

Little Toad watched a big drop of rain fall off the cabbage leaf. He smiled, remembering Woolly Bear's forecast, and gradually his eyes closed, too. It had been a long day.

Monique the caterpillar becomes a Monarch butterfly.